two lions

Published by Two Lions, New York

www.apub.com

Amazon, the Amazon logo, and Two Lions
are trademarks of Amazon.com, Inc., or its affiliates.

Library of Congress Control Number: 2014933246
ISBN-13: 9781477847770
ISBN-10: 1477847774

The illustrations are rendered in watercolor, colored pencil, graphite,
pen and ink, ballpoint pen, charcoal, and Adobe Photoshop.

Book design by Vera Soki

Printed in China
First edition

To Mom and Dad.
Thanks again, Sam!

Ohhhhh!!!
Arrrt!

But wait . . .

What IS art?

It's something a mouse like you wouldn't understand. See, I'm a true artist. I have skill and imagination.

I have skill. I can smell garbage a mile away. And I have imagination! Could *I* be a true artist?

Ha! You, an artist?

That's hard to imagine. But okay, Rudy,
if you insist. Try to paint a self-portrait.
A self-portrait is a picture you make of
yourself. Find some art supplies and start
painting.

A self-portrait, huh?

Just gotta paint myself. Easy.

Oh no! That doesn't look like me at all!

Try a still life. A still life is when you paint some things that you can put on a table – like this.

I'll paint . . . a soup can!
I guess that is a little better . . .

. . . but who would ever want
to look at a can of soup?

Try a landscape, Rudy. That's a painting of mountains or the beach or a lake . . . just about anything outside in nature.

Good idea, Claude! There's a
beautiful lake right here in the city.
I'll take a walk and see what I can paint.

Now what are you working on? That looks like something I could do!

This is found art. That's when you take objects you find and make something new.

I'm going to find some objects and
try to make my own found art!

Ta-da!

All this hard work is really making me hungry.

This garbage sure smells delicious.
Maybe I'll just have a quick nibble.

How's your found art
sculpture coming along?

Oh, Claude, I ate it!
I'll *never* be a true artist.

Rudy, why don't you borrow this book full of true artists? It will give you some new ideas.

That's it – I just needed the right look! Now I can really make a masterpiece.

And soon I'll be . . .

a true ar-

-arr-arrr-

Ahhhh!

Gah!

Whoa!

Ouch!

What have I done? I've made a huge mess.

I'm a total failure!

I'll never understand ART!

NEVER!